Put Beginning Readers on the Right Track with
ALL ABOARD READING™

The All Aboard Reading series is especially designed for beginning readers. Written by noted authors and illustrated in full color, these are books that children really want to read—books to excite their imagination, expand their interests, make them laugh, and support their feelings. With fiction and nonfiction stories that are high interest and curriculum-related, All Aboard Reading books offer something for every young reader. And with four different reading levels, the All Aboard Reading series lets you choose which books are most appropriate for your children and their growing abilities.

Picture Readers
Picture Readers have super-simple texts, with many nouns appearing as rebus pictures. At the end of each book are 24 flash cards—on one side is a rebus picture; on the other side is the written-out word.

Station Stop 1
Station Stop 1 books are best for children who have just begun to read. Simple words and big type make these early reading experiences more comfortable. Picture clues help children to figure out the words on the page. Lots of repetition throughout the text helps children to predict the next word or phrase—an essential step in developing word recognition.

Station Stop 2
Station Stop 2 books are written specifically for children who are reading with help. Short sentences make it easier for early readers to understand what they are reading. Simple plots and simple dialogue help children with reading comprehension.

Station Stop 3
Station Stop 3 books are perfect for children who are reading alone. With longer text and harder words, these books appeal to children who have mastered basic reading skills. More complex stories captivate children who are ready for more challenging books.

In addition to All Aboard Reading books, look for All Aboard Math Readers™ (fiction stories that teach math concepts children are learning in school) and All Aboard Science Readers™ (nonfiction books that explore the most fascinating science topics in age-appropriate language).

All Aboard for happy reading!

D1025719

Library of Congress Cataloging-in-Publication Data

Bryant, Megan E.
    The berry big storm / by Megan E. Bryant ; illustrated by Margo Querol and Celestino Santanach.
        p. cm. — (All aboard reading)
    "Strawberry Shortcake."
    Summary: Strawberry and her friends clean up after a rainstorm that causes the River Fudge to flood. [1. Rain and rainfall—Fiction. 2. Friendship—Fiction.] I. Querol, Margo, ill. II. Santanach, Celestino, ill. III. Title. IV. Series.
    PZ7.B83945 Be 2003
    [E]—dc21

ISBN 0-448-43135-1 (pb)   C D E F G H I J

ALL ABOARD READING™

Station Stop 1

The Berry Big Storm

By Megan E. Bryant
Illustrated by Margo Querol
and Celestino Santanach

Grosset & Dunlap • New York

It rains all day
in Strawberryland.

It rains all night
in Strawberryland.

It rains all <u>week</u> in Strawberryland!

What a <u>berry</u> big storm!

Strawberry Shortcake hopes
her friends are okay.

Strawberry Shortcake
and Apple Dumplin'
and their pets
get ready to go outside.

They put on their raincoats.

They put on their rain boots.

They get their umbrellas.

11

They go to see
Huckleberry Pie.

Oh, no!

Too much rain!

The River Fudge is rising!

The roof is leaking!

Huckleberry needs help.

What a <u>berry</u> big mess!

Pupcake and Custard
get some friends to help.

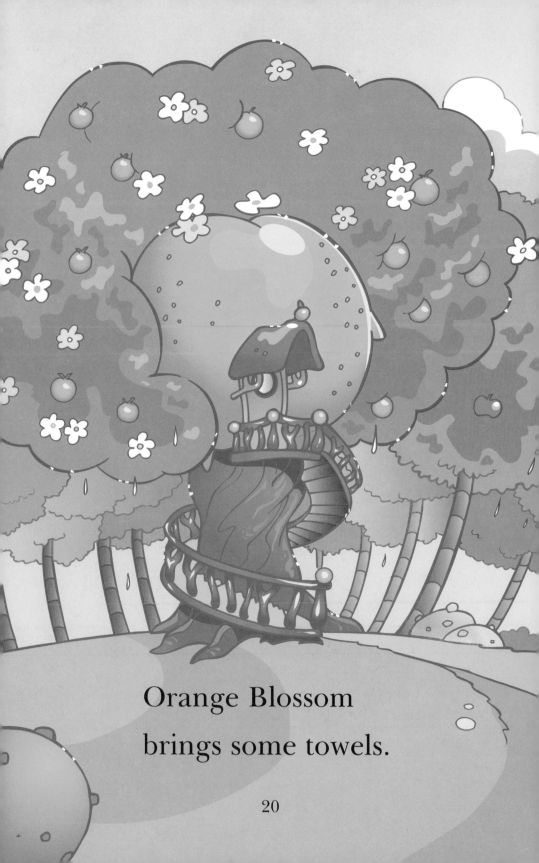

Orange Blossom

brings some towels.

Ginger Snap
brings some tools.

Angel Cake

brings some bags.

And some treats!

Time to fix the roof.

Time to bag the river.

Time to clean up.

Time to eat treats!

Kids have fun
and work gets done
when friends help out.
<u>Berry</u> good job, everybody!